Disney
THE LITTLE MERMAID
I AM ARIEL

Disney
PRINCESS

Twin Tales

Two Great Stories...
One Great Book!

I am a Princess

AUTUMN
PUBLISHING

AUTUMN
PUBLISHING

Published in 2021
First published in the UK by Autumn Publishing
An imprint of Igloo Books Ltd
Cottage Farm, NN6 0BJ, UK
Owned by Bonnier Books
Sveavägen 56, Stockholm, Sweden
www.igloobooks.com

© 2021 Disney Enterprises, Inc.

1221 001
2 4 6 8 10 9 7 5 3 1
ISBN 978-1-80022-320-2

Printed and manufactured in China

This book belongs to:

....

I am
Ariel.

I live under the sea in the kingdom of…

… Atlantica.

My father is King Triton.
He rules all the **merpeople.**

I have six sisters.
Their names are
**Alana, Aquata.
Andrina, Attina,
Arista** and
Adella.

I'm the youngest.

Being a mermaid is fun! I get to sing with the **royal orchestra**...

... conducted by **Sebastian** the crab...

... and go exploring with my best friend **Flounder**.

Do you want to know **a secret?**
As much fun as it is to be a **mermaid**, I'd really rather be **human!**

I enjoy learning all I can about the human world. **Scuttle** the seagull teaches me things.

Sometimes – even though I am not supposed to –
I swim to the surface to watch humans.

I think humans are wonderful. Especially
the one called **Prince Eric!**

I like to **collect objects** I find in **shipwrecks**. All my treasures used to belong to humans.

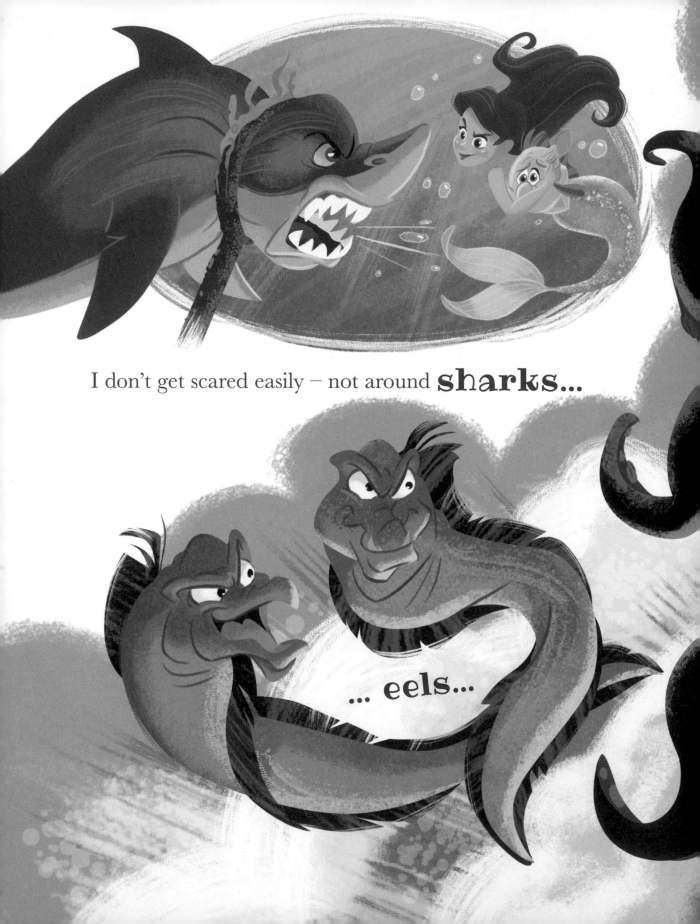

I don't get scared easily – not around **sharks...**

... eels...

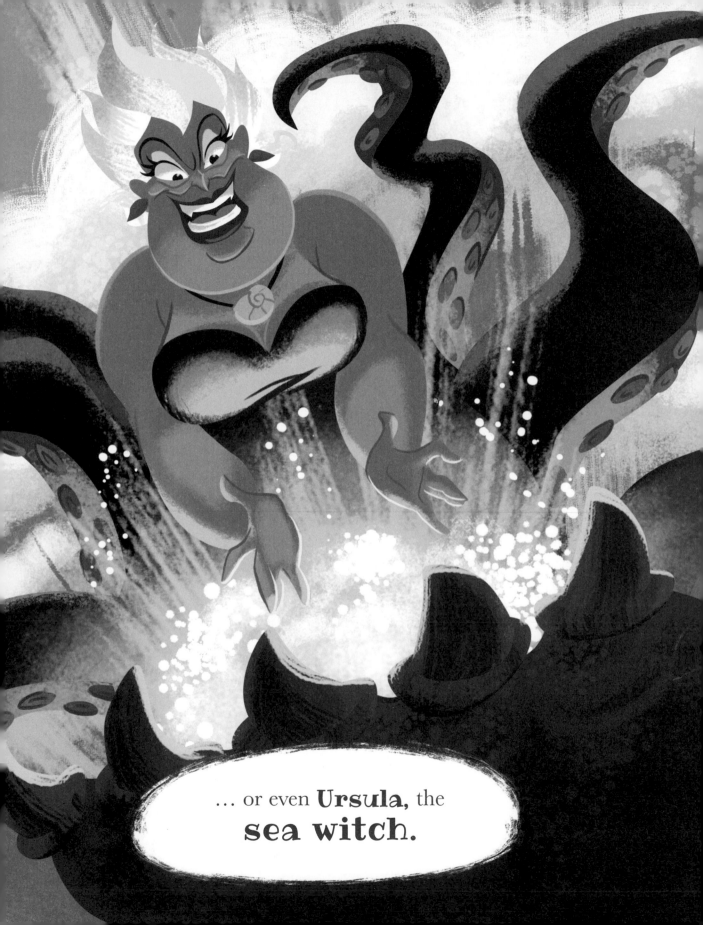

... or even **Ursula**, the
sea witch.

When I want something badly enough,
I don't give up.

I made a deal with Ursula. In
exchange for my voice, she made
me human for a few days.

Swimming without a tail is **hard!**

I **love** my new legs!

… and that **music** helps make every moment **special**.

I am so thankful my father used his magical trident to make me human —

this time forever.

I get to be with Eric and still stay close to my merfamily. Now I have the **best of both worlds!**

Disney PRINCESS

I am a Princess

Hello! My name is Cinderella. I am a princess.
I live in a beautiful castle and have lots of fancy gowns and jewels. But not all princesses are the same – we each enjoy doing our own special thing.

I love caring for animals…

... and having them care for me!

Hello! I am Snow White.

I like to have fun with my friends
Happy, Sleepy, Sneezy, Grumpy,
Doc, Bashful and Dopey…

... and then surprise them with a sweet treat.

My name is Tiana, and I love to cook!

Even when I was a frog, I made a tasty gumbo for my friends Prince Naveen, Louis and Ray.

Now I get to make lots of people happy with my food – at my very own restaurant!

Hello! I am Rapunzel.

I love to paint pictures...

… and play with Pascal. He is really good at hide-and-seek!

My name is Aurora.

When I was a baby, I was given
the gift of song, so I love music.

Now I enjoy dancing with Prince Phillip
whenever we get the chance!

My name is Jasmine.

I love going on adventures with Aladdin beside me!

Bonjour! I am Belle.

I love to read all kinds of books.

I even like to read about other princesses.
Don't you?